ANT an.
Go Sho

CW00847512

written and illustrated by Angela Banner

EGMONT

This **ANT and BEE** book
belongs to

. . . .

. . . .

One day Ant and Bee needed to
make a shopping list because
Kind Dog was coming to supper.

5

Ant and Bee wrote their shopping list on a piece of paper that was square and flat.

7

Ant and Bee cut the square and
flat piece of paper in half, so they
each had a half of the square
and flat shopping list.

LIST

APPLE PIE	CAKE
GRAPES	BANANAS
NUTS	CRISPS
BALL	BISCUIT
(FOR KIND DOG)	BONE
	(FOR KIND DOG)

Then Ant went
to his money bank.
It was . . . square and fat.

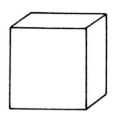

And Bee went
to his money bank.
It was . . . round and fat.

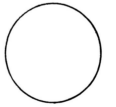

11

Ant and Bee each took five round and flat money coins out of their money banks.

THIS BOX BELONGS TO **ANT**

BACK OF SQUARE BOX MONEY BANK

BACK OF ROUND BALL MONEY BANK

PEEP HOLE FOR GLOATING

13

Then Ant and Bee put the two halves of the square and flat shopping list inside their shopping basket.

The basket had a balloon that was round and fat.

Then OFF flew Ant and Bee to a big shop that was . . .

... square **and** round **and** fat **and** flat!

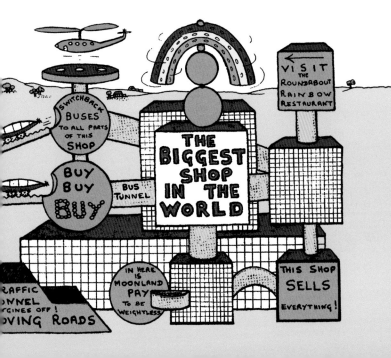

Bee told Ant before they went inside the shop that they must only buy what was written on their shopping lists because . . .

. . . they only had enough
money to buy what was
written on their shopping lists.

BUT Ant tried to buy lots of things that were not written on his shopping list . . . so Bee told Ant to give back all his wrong shopping.

23

Then Ant did his proper shopping

. . . for lots of round things.

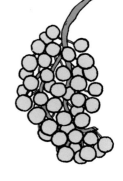

An apple pie,   grapes,

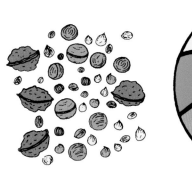

nuts,　　　　　a ball for Kind Dog.

Then Bee did all his shopping

. . . for different-shaped things.

A cake,   bananas,

crisps,   a chew biscuit

for Kind Dog.

All these things . . .

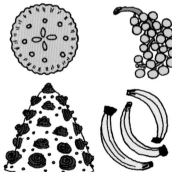

. . . cost all this money.

Ant and Bee had spent nine

round and flat money coins.

29

Bee said they must spend their last round and flat money coin

on a pink square shopping bag.

Ant said the pink square shopping bag was not as good as their old shopping basket, but Bee wanted the pink square shopping bag.

Ant said NO!
Bee said YES!
Ant said NO!
Bee said YES!

Bee bought the pink square shopping bag with their last round and flat money coin and put all the shopping inside.

Then Bee flew home . . .

. . . with Ant.

BUT

when Ant and Bee came home,
they saw that a most terrible thing
had happened.

All their shopping was
SQUASHED
because the pink square shopping
bag was not as good for carrying
shopping as their old basket.

When Kind Dog came to supper Ant and Bee were still crying.

So Kind Dog told Ant and Bee to be happy again because they could still have a very nice supper party with squashed food.

42

The squashed food looked funny
but it tasted very nice.

43

After supper Kind Dog asked Ant and Bee to go shopping with him the next day.

Kind Dog said he wanted to give Ant and Bee a very happy shopping time.

Ant and Bee said YES.

The next day Kind Dog said the Zoo Man had given him ten round and flat money coins for them to spend!

 Kind Dog told Ant and Bee that they must buy fruit, cakes and chocolates!

Then Ant and Bee made a new shopping list.

47

CHOCOLATES

FRUIT

LIST

CAKES

48

Ant and Bee cut the square and flat piece of paper into three pieces . . . and then Ant and Bee and Kind Dog each had their own shopping list. Kind Dog was very happy to take Ant and Bee shopping . . .

. . . to the shop that
Kind Dog liked best!

Kind Dog said they must go

and choose some cakes.

52

Ant chose a round and flat cake.

Bee chose a square and fat cake.

Kind Dog chose a cake that was

round and square and flat and fat!

CAKES

STICKY BUNS

ROUND AND FLAT CAKES | SQUARE AND FAT CAKES | SQUARE AND FLAT CAKES | ROUND AND FAT CAKES

55

Kind Dog told Ant and Bee NOT TO WORRY about the cakes getting squashed as the shop would pack the cakes into square and fat empty boxes.

After buying the cakes, Ant and
Bee and Kind Dog went to buy
some plums!

The shop put their three soft
plums safely inside empty boxes.

Then Ant and Bee went to buy
a chocolate mountain, chocolate
beans and a chocolate log.

The shop put the chocolates
very carefully into empty boxes.

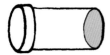 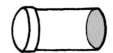 

CAKES. FRUIT. CHOCOLATES.

All the shopping was done!

The shopping had cost six

round and flat money coins.

Suddenly Kind Dog ran away with
the four round and flat money
coins that had not been spent.

Ant and Bee asked the shop
to send out a message telling
Kind Dog that they were waiting
for him in the waiting room.
WHERE WAS KIND DOG?

Kind Dog was not in the part of
the shop that sold BEDS.

66

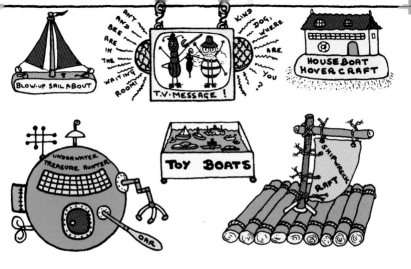

Kind Dog was not in the part of

the shop that sold BOATS.

Kind Dog was not in the part of
the shop that sold BIRDS.

Kind Dog was in the part of the
shop that sold BARGAINS.

When Kind Dog came back to
Ant and Bee he had spent the
four round and flat money coins
on two secret parcels!

YOU HAVE JUST LEFT
THE
BEST
BIG SHOP
GOODBYE

PLEASE COME AGAIN
xxx

Then they all
went home.

AND NOTHING WAS SQUASHED!

Then they had a party with
cakes and fruit and chocolates
and the two secret parcels.

CHEAP !!
ODD SIZES
BOTH SKATES FOR
2 COINS ONLY!

COSTS ONLY
2 COINS

BRICKS

SOME
MISSING

77

Ant and Bee made all this with
their bricks!

And the skate went safely over the bump!